APPALACHIAN GHOSTS

Other books by the author

GHOSTS AND SPECTERS
AMERICA'S MOST HAUNTED PLACES
GHOSTS OF THE WILD WEST

APPALACHIAN GHOSTS

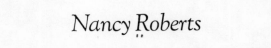

Nancy Roberts

Photographs by Bruce Roberts

DOUBLEDAY & COMPANY, INC.
GARDEN CITY, NEW YORK

Library of Congress Cataloging in Publication Data

Roberts, Nancy, 1924–
Appalachian ghosts.

CONTENTS: Laura.—The coming of the demon.—
The letter.—The ghost fiddlers.—The haunted
copper mine.   [etc.]
1. Ghosts—Appalachian region.   I. Title.
BF1472.U6R63   133.1′29′75

ISBN 0-385-12294-2 Trade
0-385-12295-0 Prebound
Library of Congress Catalog Card Number 77–76263
Copyright © 1978 by Bruce and Nancy Roberts
Printed in the United States of America
All Rights Reserved
FIRST EDITION

Contents

Laura

THE afternoon was gray and misty, not the kind that Larry Huff would usually choose for a motorcycle ride. But he had just traded in his old motorcycle for a new Honda—bought himself a new jacket—and the temptation to take off was irresistible.

When he sped down Highway 55 out of Campbellsville, Kentucky, and headed south toward Columbia, he had no premonition of what lay in store for him.

It was a great ride, with the cool, moist air blowing in his face as he swooped around the curves. There were almost no cars on the road. In fact, he must have gone five miles before he met one. In some places the fog made it difficult to see for any distance ahead but there were often foggy places along this road and Larry didn't really mind.

She waited for him beside the road in the rain and the fog.

It gave him a feeling of being in another world—a world of fluffy whiteness and, above all, quiet. He liked that, for in the small house where he lived with his parents and four brothers and sisters, there was often so much noise that there was no chance to think. He wasn't sure just what it was that he wanted to be alone to think about, but sometimes he grew angry inside when the clamor of voices made his thoughts so jerky that he couldn't make sense out of whatever was gnawing on him at the moment. He could put things together when he rode alone like this.

Instead of the weather clearing, a slow, drizzling rain began to fall, but Larry still did not want to turn back. As he rounded one of the curves, a small, single tree near a clump of trees on his right appeared to move. But when he approached, he saw it was a thin-looking girl wearing a cloak walking beside the road.

He stopped to ask if there was anything he could do for her, she looked so cold and forlorn, her hair clinging wetly about her cheeks, her dress long and bedraggled. At first he thought she was not going to answer, but she replied, "Well, if you don't mind, I'd like to have a ride down the road a piece to my house." By now the drizzle had changed to a light rain and Larry offered her his new jacket. She put it on gratefully and climbed up behind him on the motorcycle, winding her arms about his waist. He was conscious of the cold from her hands penetrating even through his shirt. The ride was not a comfortable one as her grip gradually grew tighter, and his back felt cold as ice.

They were near Cane Valley when she spoke up and pointed to a house set back from the highway. "That's where I live," she said and Larry turned up the road toward it. It was an old farmhouse and the girl muttered a quick, "Thank you," ran up the front steps and in the door, closing it behind her. Larry was so glad not to have her holding on with those cold hands around his waist that he hurriedly took off.

It was not until he was part way home that he remembered his new jacket, but by then it was getting quite dark and he had no desire to return to the farmhouse at night.

Next morning he headed back down Highway 55 toward Cane Valley and when he reached the girl's house he went up and knocked on the front door, thinking she might answer it. A woman came to the door instead, so he described the girl and said he had lent her his jacket.

The woman's eyes filled with tears. "I don't know how you've done it. You've described just how my girl, Laura, looked, but she's been dead seven years."

Larry stared at her in disbelief. "Ma'am, I just can't believe it. She was as real as can be and I could even feel how wet and cold she was."

"Wait a minute. I'd like for you to go with me," said the woman. She went into the house and got her coat and he followed her to the back and up to the top of a hill where there was a small family cemetery surrounded by a fence. As she opened the gate, he was surprised to see something was hanging over the top of a tombstone on the far side.

When they reached it he was amazed. His jacket was draped over the tombstone and below it, engraved on the stone, was the name "LAURA." The date was seven years ago. He reclaimed the jacket but it was too damp to put on, even if he had wanted to.

Although he kept the coat for several years, he never seemed able to wear it, for always, after he had worn it for a few minutes, it would begin to feel cold and wet and he would have to take it off. The jacket still looked like new but finally one night, after trying again to wear it, he became angry and threw it in the fire.

A strange odor suffused the room like the scent of flowers massed around a freshly dug grave. Larry was so terrified he ran out of the house into the night.

Even now as he tells the story, his face turns white, his eyes fill with horror and he will never ride down Highway 55 on a foggy, rainy day again.

The Coming of the Demon

ADAM LIVINGSTONE was an honest, religious man and a hard-working farmer. It is hard to realize how a man like this can become involved with a demon, and yet that is what happened.

Near the beginning of the nineteenth century Livingstone and his wife came down to what later became West Virginia from Pennsylvania and purchased a lakeside farm near the town that is now Middleway. It was then called Smithfield and later Wizard Clip. This last name came from the series of disasters that happened to the Livingstone family.

In front of their farm and beside the Opequon River ran the wagon route from Baltimore to southwest Virginia, Kentucky, and Tennessee. During the day, wagon after

wagon rattled along the road and Livingstone would sell
or barter his farm produce with the wagon drivers.

One bitterly cold November night the event befell the
Livingstones that was to lead to a terrifying series of hap-
penings, although it appeared quite commonplace at the
time. During these days there were few inns with accom-
modations for travelers and they often stopped at a house
and asked if they might spend the night.

The Livingstones were in bed listening to the rain and
wind outside when they heard a pounding on their front

The dogwoods bloomed in the happy days before the demon
came to the Livingstone home.

In front of the Livingstone farm and beside the Opequon River ran the wagon route from Baltimore to southwest Virginia, Kentucky, and Tennessee.

door. Adam went down to see who it could be. He cautiously opened the door a few inches but the force of the wind was such that it tore the door from his hand and flung it open revealing a black hole in the outer darkness. In the midst of it stood a tall stranger, his cloak billowing in the wind.

"My wagon wheel is broken and I am not able to have it repaired until morning," said the stranger. "I would like to ask for a night's lodging, sir, and I assure you I will pay you generously."

"We have an extra room and you are welcome to it," replied Livingstone. "My wife has gone to bed or I would ask her to prepare food for you, but let me show you to your room."

The stranger appeared grateful and followed him up the steep, winding stairs to a room which was sparsely furnished but had a comfortable feather bed. Although he wore the clothes of a gentleman, Livingstone took his usual precaution of locking the door at the foot of the stairs. This was a common practice when a family lodged strangers on the second floor for the night.

The Livingstones heard the man walk about the room. They heard his boots hit the floor one by one and then the bed creaked. Leaving only the candle burning by their bed, they were soon asleep. A short time later they were awakened by the sound of a terrible moaning and groaning above them, punctuated now and then by a sharp outcry of pain. It was the traveler.

Taking the bedside candle, Livingstone unlocked the door to the stairs and went up to see what was the matter. He found his guest tossing in his bed and deathly ill. The man told him he did not expect to live to see daylight, and he asked if Livingstone would summon a Catholic priest to give him the last rites, admitting that he had neglected his religion in health but now felt need of its consolation.

Livingstone told him that there was no priest nearby nor could he hope to find one closer than Maryland but that he would ask his neighbors, the McSherrys and the Minghinis, who were Catholic and perhaps they could tell him of one. Mrs. Livingstone had come up, and as she listened to the conversation she began to grow angry.

"Surely, you are not going out on any such wild-goose chase on a night like this. The best thing we can do is go back to bed, and I'll wager this guest of ours will be as well as you or I by morning."

But the Livingstones could not sleep the rest of the night, for there were the most pitiful cries and pleas coming from the room above. Finally, just before day came, all was quiet. About eight o'clock when they heard no sound, Livingstone went up. Their guest was dead. It was then that they realized they did not know his name and couldn't find it in any of his belongings. Mrs. Livingstone told the neighbors a traveler had asked to lodge with them the night before and had died in his sleep. She did not mention his begging them to summon a priest. The funeral was a simple one, held late the following afternoon.

After the Livingstones returned to their home, Adam built a fire and they sat down before it to warm themselves. Suddenly, the logs in the fireplace began to writhe and twist so violently that they erupted from the fireplace into a fiery dance around the room. Livingstone ran from one to the other trying to catch them and put them back but as soon as he did they would fly out again. This went on for almost an hour and they were terrified. When the dancing finally stopped, the Livingstones were too frightened to sleep.

Tired as Livingstone was, he went down to the road

with some of his produce the next morning and was surprised to hear a wagon driver cursing at him. The man's team of oxen had stopped in the middle of the road.

"Take that rope down! What are you doing, tying a rope across a public road?" the angry man shouted. The exhausted and bewildered Livingstone could see no rope at all and he thought the man must be drunk. The driver took out a large knife and began slashing the air with it. To his amazement the knife met no resistance. Livingstone suggested that he drive on. He did and the wagon went through. What a shame for a man to be drunk so early in the day, thought Livingstone. It was only a short time, however, before another wagon came clattering down the road with a load of pots and pans and the same thing happened. The driver pulled to a stop so quickly that several of the pans fell banging and rattling to the ground. Then he started to shout about a rope, and shook his fist at Livingstone. Finally, he was persuaded to drive on, but similar incidents kept up for several weeks.

By now the Livingstones and their neighbors, who had all noticed these strange events, were sure that they were the work of some supernatural power. Each day brought new and frightening phenomena. Showers of stones would strike the Livingstone house, articles of furniture would topple over, balls of fire rolled over the floor without any apparent cause. But most frequent was a sharp clipping noise as if made by gigantic, invisible shears which could be heard in and around the house, and crescent shaped slits began to appear in the family clothes and table linen.

Mrs. Livingstone and a lady visitor were sitting on the porch talking and the lady commented on the fine flock of ducks waddling through the yard on the way to the river. She had no sooner spoken than the uncanny, invisible shears went "Clip-clip, clip-clip!" and one after another

After the demon arrived, the field behind the Livingstone home seemed always to be shrouded in fog.

each duck's head fell to the ground before the horrified la-
dies' eyes.

The young men of the neighborhood talked Livingstone
into letting them hold a dance at his home. One boastful
fellow brought his rifle and bragged about all he would do
if "the Clipper" came near him. For a while everything
went smoothly, but right in the middle of one of the
dances the fellow who had been boasting began yelling
wildly. There was the sound of huge, demoniacal scissors
whacking through cloth. The boaster grasped his britches
which were now flapping around the back of his legs and
ran through the nearest door.

That night, after the dance was over, Livingstone had a
strange dream. He dreamed he was standing at the foot of
a hill looking up at a man in flowing black robes who was
conducting a religious ceremony. As he watched, a voice
spoke saying, "I am the man who can rid you of the
demon." He was much astonished and decided the man in
his dream was a priest so he decided to attend Catholic
services nearby at Sheperdstown. He went with his Catholic
neighbors, and the moment he saw the priest he recognized
the man he had seen in his dream.

Tears streaming down his face, he poured out the story
of his heartless treatment of the stranger, the weird chain
of events that had followed, and he begged for help. Father Cahill was a big-fisted Irishman who was not afraid of
the devil himself and he accompanied Livingstone back
home. There he got down on his knees and prayed, and
sprinkled holy water on the threshold of the house.

"Now, I want you to take me to the place where the
stranger was buried," said the priest, and together they
went to an old cemetery. Livingstone showed him the
grave and the priest began to consecrate it. As he did so,

the wind rose, leaves rustled, and small trees started to
sway. But along with the wind sounds there was another
that grew and swelled until it became a dreadful sort of
moan. Livingstone was terribly frightened. He looked at
the dark waters of the nearby lake tossing tumultuously. In
a few minutes the moan faded and the waters grew still,
perhaps, because they had taken back their own.

After that day, there were no more signs of the demon·
at the Livingstone home, and Adam Livingstone was so
grateful that he deeded thirty-four acres of his farm to the
Catholic church. The deed may be seen today, recorded on
the yellowing pages of an old book in the County Clerk's
office at Charles Town, West Virginia. The land is a half
mile or so west of the main turnpike through Middleway.
The soil is poor, and shattered limestone rock is close to
the surface. For many years the foundation of an ancient
house could be seen. Many have claimed to hear the hoof
beats of a galloping horse there, and on dark and blustery
autumn nights they talk of a figure in a billowing cape
striding toward the small chapel, built on the spot by the
Catholic church, and disappearing within. Is it the spirit of
the stranger returning to give thanks at being released
from this earth by the priest? No one really knows.

The Letter

JAMES RAMSAY stood in the fading sunlight. He was surrounded by the bodies of the Confederate dead and, who knows, perhaps their spirits. The battle of South Mountain was over, for the Confederates had come out of a thin line of woods scarcely two hours before, helpless and with empty muskets. His own New York regiment, taking cruel advantage of the situation, had shot them down as they stood there not twenty feet away.

Most of the dead Confederates were from the coastal district of North Carolina. They wore "butternut" uniforms, the color ranging all the way from deep coffee-brown to the whitish brown of ordinary dust. He looked down into the poor, pinched faces, worn with marching and scant fare and his anger toward them died. There was no "secession" in those rigid forms nor in those fixed eyes staring blankly at the sky. It was not "their" war anymore.

Sone of the Union soldiers were taking the finer powder from the cartridge boxes of the dead and priming their muskets with it. Except for that, each body lay untouched as it had fallen. Darkness came on quickly before there was time to bury the dead. Ramsay and his comrades unrolled the blankets of the rebels and went about covering each body. The air was full of the fragrance of pennyroyal, an herb bruised by the tramping of a hundred feet, and he would always remember it as part of this day.

It was Sunday, September 14, 1862, but the air was chilly, and after munching on some of their cooked rations and listening to the firing which continued until about nine o'clock that evening, the men drew their blankets over them and went to sleep. It was a strange sight, thought Ramsay. Stretched out here in the narrow field lay living Yankee and dead Confederate, side by side, nor could one be told from the other.

Sometime after midnight, James Ramsay awoke very thirsty. He reached for his water flask to find it empty, and then he recalled that he had forgotten to fill it at the stream. He must have said this aloud to himself for the figure next to him rose on one elbow and extended his own water flask. Ramsay drank from it gratefully, thanked him, and was about to lie back upon his arms when a voice said, "I have a letter in my breast pocket. Would you see that it gets to my wife?"

"Of course," replied Ramsay, and exhausted he fell asleep once more. He awoke at daylight as he had for so many dawns during the past few months and began to recall where he was and what had happened the day before while he waited for the rest of the camp to stir. Then he remembered his buddy next to him who had given him a

When he awoke in the morning, the guns were silent and flowers were blooming amid the pennyroyal.

He had the letter in his pocket given him by the ghost of the dead Confederate.

drink during the night. What was it the man had said? He had asked him to carry a letter to his wife, that was it. Poor fellow. Like all of them, he knew that each day might so easily be his last. Ramsay glanced over at him curiously to see who it was.

Then he realized that the man on his right was not from his own regiment but was one of the dead Confederates they had not had time to bury the night before. It must be the fellow asleep on the other side, then. He turned. This, too, was a dead Confederate. Nor was there any water flask on the body.

He could not believe his eyes. He was certain it had been no dream for he clearly remembered the man raising up to give him water. One thing would tell him. He peeled the blanket back from the Confederate and reached into his breast pocket. In it was a letter addressed to "Mrs. John Carpenter." He opened it and began to read: "My dearest wife, I think of you daily and in the event I am not able to return to tell you, I want you to know that . . ."

Ramsay read no further. He was not a superstitious man, but he knew that his experience was too real to discount. He would never forget the night he had met the spirit of a Confederate soldier named John Carpenter as they slept side by side in a field in Maryland.

The Ghost Fiddlers

THERE is an old house in West Virginia that only comes alive at night. That is, if you can say that a house inhabited by spirits can come "alive."

The old log cabin leaned forward and seemed to stare menacingly. Its supports sagged. A door hung from one hinge. The young couple stood for a moment and stared back. Then the man walked over to look at the steps.

"Pretty good shape. This 'uns a house with good timber and we can make it right."

"Oh, Peter, this old house scares me just to look at it."

"Scares you?"

"Yes, there's something wrong about it. There'll never be anything but sadness in it."

"You're not thinkin' straight, Sarry. Yer family lets the

The ghost fiddlers' cabin.

tunes from all that fiddlin' make 'em feel all sorts a crazy things. Now, remember, I don't never want none of that fiddlin' in our home."

Sarry's eyes looked hurt, but she gave a reluctant little nod. She was a pretty girl who loved to sing and dance, and she was from a family of fiddle players. The girls could play about as well as the men. But Peter Barton thought the fiddle was the instrument of the devil, for that's the way he was raised. Music led a body away from things they ought to be doing, like serving the Lord, and could make him forget he would soon be standing before the judgment seat.

Peter had wanted to preach but had worked so hard there was no time to practice at it. But my, what a powerful prayer he could make! Lots of folks went to preachin' just to hear Peter Barton pray.

He began to repair the house and sometimes Sarry would come out bringing some of the yellow rosebushes from her homeplace to plant to keep it from looking so desolate.

It was a somber wedding with no music, for Sarry's dad and brothers knew better than to fetch any fiddles along. A year later a boy was born. Peter wanted to call him after one of the thundering prophets of the Old Testament, but Sarry said her grandpappy's name, James, was the same as one of the apostles' and her husband agreed. They lived to themselves, for Peter never wanted to take her over to see his family, for that instrument of the devil, the fiddle, could often be heard, its strains floating from the cabin at night. Secretly, Peter feared he might come to like one of the gay tunes or plaintive lover's ballads and then he was convinced he would lose his faith.

Folks passing the Barton house at suppertime could hear Peter's strong, resonant voice reciting the blessing as if he were giving a benediction to the multitude. He took Sarry and the boy to church and never missed a meeting. People said the prayers he prayed could make chills run down a man's spine. Somehow, he never had any close friends, for he didn't seem to trust anybody. Some said it was because he'd had to scrabble so hard for what he'd got. They also said he was a strong-tempered man and that both Sarry and the boy were afraid of him.

Sarry's ma took sick one day and they sent for Sarry, so Peter took her and the boy, James, on their two white mules. Right off, James saw a fiddle hanging on the wall and asked his granddaddy what it was for. It was the first time he'd ever seen one. His granddaddy took it down and played a gay, lilting melody. James wanted to try it but his father scowled and the boy was afraid to touch it. When they left, Peter told James that he was never to play such an instrument of the devil and if he ever took it up, he'd have to leave home.

Sometimes Peter would make money by running a raft of logs down the river. There was much timber in the area and he would tie the loose logs into a raft and ride it downstream where he would sell them to buy land. It took about four days because he would have to walk back. One day while he was gone, James's grandmother became sick again and he and his mother went over to the house. He asked his granddad to play for him, and when he had finished James wanted to try it. Sarry's father suggested she take the fiddle home with her and teach the boy while his father was away.

Sarry looked at the fiddle with longing and all the beautiful, haunting melodies she had learned as a girl came to mind. How she had missed them! She couldn't resist, and from then on she and James would play when his father was away.

One morning Peter told them good-by and set out for
the river to run a raft of logs downstream and sell the timber.

"The water's pretty high, Sarry, and it may take me
longer to get back, for some of the small streams are going
to get higher if it rains some more. I may have trouble
gettin' acrost them on foot, but I'm aimin' to get back in
about four days."

Sarry did her chores. James chopped some wood,
planted taters in the garden, and it was late afternoon
when he finished. That night after supper his mother saw
him look up toward the loft where they had the fiddle hid-
den. Her eyes met his and she nodded her head, "Go
ahead, Jamie." He played while his mother sat listening in
the old rocking chair her Pa had given her. Every now and
then she would take the fiddle herself and play a tune.
The two of them had such a good time they paid no mind
to the late hour.

Meanwhile, Peter had set out down the river but the
water was high, and about ten miles from home he
reached a spot where the river narrowed and curved. Here
the current was swift and it pulled the raft right over the
big rocks he had always managed to see and avoid when
the water was lower. The raft went all to pieces and only
by clinging to one of the logs was he able to keep from
drowning. He stopped at a house to dry himself and by
the time he had walked all the way home, it was getting
on toward midnight. He was suprised to see the light of a
lamp burning in the little cabin, but as he drew closer he
knew why. The wind brought the sound of a gay, foot-tap-
ping melody called "Sweet Sunny Sal." Peter's face grew
grim and hard. The appealing lilt of the tune, rather than
touch his heart, only moved him to anger.

A fiddle was used at dances and other frolics. It was

clearly the instrument of the devil in the eyes of the mountain preachers, and Peter flung open the door in a black rage. He snatched the fiddle out of Jamie's hands and taking his knife he deliberately cut every string. Then he hung it near the mantel and turned to Jamie, thundering, "There hangs the instrument of the devil as a reminder to all them who would not obey. I told you, Jamie, you'd have to leave this house if you ever brought a fiddle into it. Now, you go to your grandpappy's and stay there."

Jamie had no light, but he was afraid of his father and he left right then. Sarry thought he would go to her Pa's place and stay there 'til Peter cooled down and then come back. But that was not to be.

The following morning Peter rose early to milk the cow. She was in the far pasture and when he went to fetch her, he saw a dark crumpled figure lying at the foot of the cliff at one side of the field. It was Jamie. He had lost his footing in the dark, fallen down the cliff head first, and struck a stump. The boy's neck was broken. Peter carried his son's body back to the house.

It is said that Peter was never the same. He no longer took his logs down the river. He scarcely talked to anyone now, and in church he never prayed aloud again. Four years later he was killed when one of the mules kicked him, splitting his head open. Some folks said he had told Sarry he would live only four years, one year for each string he had cut on the fiddle. He was buried beside his son in the graveyard.

Sarry lived on at the house getting queerer and queerer, and late at night when folks walked the path near the cabin they would hear the strains of a fiddle playing. One morning someone found her sitting in her rocking chair with a fiddle across her lap and a smile upon her face. Stranger still, even after the old lady died, the sounds kept on and, if anything, there were more and more reports of music rippling through the night air coming from the old cabin, sometimes gay but more often sad and plaintive.

Even today there are few people who care to walk the path near the old cabin after dark, nor does anyone want to stay over night or live there again. It is a dark, sagging skeleton of a place. Yet they say that near midnight the eerie, haunting music of Jamie's fiddle may still be heard— coming from beyond the grave.

Sometimes the old house seems to come alive and the sound of eerie music can be heard.

The Haunted Copper Mine

JACK McCAULLA had worked in the mines all his life and, as his friends used to say, "There ain't much Jack's afeard of." Like every man who worked in the mines, Jack lived with danger, but he knew how to handle it better than most. Or so everyone thought.

The Ducktown copper mines were on the Georgia-Tennessee border and they were the only places a man could make money as good as a dollar a day in the 1890s.

Jack was working a tunnel about four hundred feet down one day when a bunch of men became scared to death. One of the engines failed that ran both the air pump, which pushed fresh air through the mine, and the wooden elevator that brought men up from the shafts. The miners ran toward the shaft and began scurrying up the steel wire ladder that hung on the solid rock wall, climbing from level to level.

. They were all crowded around the base of the ladder and some were pushing and shoving. Just as McCaulla's turn came to go up it, a panic-stricken old man thrust in ahead of him and McCaulla stood aside, letting him go up first. Jack was the last man to go up the ladder. Later his fellow miners talked about it, and when one of the mine officials asked him if it were true, he just said, "Well, we couldn't all climb that ladder at once. Someone always has to be last."

A few months later Jack McCaulla was working about four hundred feet down in the mine when he went to the end of one of the tunnels that had been blasted the day before in a pocket of rich copper-bearing ore. By the light of the lamp on his cap he began to pick up large chunks of the ore and load his mine car with the blasted-down rock.

He had been loading the car for almost an hour when he heard a peculiar hissing sound as if air were escaping from the pipe. The pipes brought the life-saving fresh air under heavy pressure along the tunnels. The sound grew louder and he began to think it might come from water running down the side of the tunnel. He stopped shoveling the ore and began to listen. As he did so he was aware of a change in the sound. No longer was it a hissing nor the noise of running water, but it was becoming more and more eerie.

It was a chorus sobbing and moaning in unison, and he recognized human voices. Somehow, he knew it was the voices of all the miners who had died in this mine and their cries were so loud they seemed to surround and overwhelm him. His hands became clammy, his face beaded with perspiration, and he didn't wait to finish loading his

Down in the mine there was a chorus of sobbing, moaning human voices.

mine car but pushed the car to the shaft as quickly as possible. The wailing seemed to follow him all the way to the skip. He rode the skip up, dumped his ore, and went to the surface boss and told him he had heard the cries of all the men who had ever been killed in this mine.

The face of the man who had long been unafraid was the color of ashes. The boss looked at him and paid him off, nor did McCaulla ever go back to work in the Isabella copper mine at Ducktown again.

The Ghost of John Henry
Lives On

Some people in Talcott, Hilldale, and Hinton, West Virginia, say the ghost of John Henry still haunts the east portal of the Big Bend Tunnel. And it is true that within days after John Henry's death, work came to a halt because laborers could still hear his hammers ringing in the tunnel.

In 1870, when the tunnel was started, John Henry was there. The tunnel was one of the most ambitious projects of its day. More than a mile long, it would cut off nine miles as it went through Big Bend Mountain and came out on the other side. The tunnel was a real man-eater, for the hard, red, shale rock through which it was driven would crumble when exposed to air and at least one out of every five workers died from rock falls in the building of it.

The steel drivers were the princes of the working crews, and John Henry was king of them all. He was a big, black man, six feet tall, two hundred pounds, superbly muscled, and an artist with his hammers. It was not easy to slam one hammer at the end of a 1½-inch-diameter drill hour after hour, day after day without missing.

Little Bill, John Henry's "turner" held the drill turning it slightly after each blow giving it a little shake to flip the rock dust out of the hole. The drills would get dull after a few minutes and while those hammers of John Henry's flew back and forth—he could swing a hammer in each hand—Little Bill would hold out a hand to the "walker" who kept getting the drills resharpened by the blacksmith at the tunnel entrance, and he'd slip another into the hole fast between hammer blows. The steel driver couldn't break the rhythm of his hammers any more than a distance runner could break his stride.

In rock drilling contests the drivers kept up a rate of ninety blows a minute and a dozen times in a fifteen-minute match. The "turner" would replace the steel drill, with bloodied flesh to pay if his timing was poor.

But the most famous contest that ever happened was when John Henry told his boss he could beat the steam drill. John Henry was a proud man. The rest of the men admired him and Banks Terry, who used to do odd jobs in the tunnel, always talked a lot about him—said he could drive steel straight ahead or straight into the roof while standing on a powder keg, never tiring, never missing a stroke, singing all the while and wearing out drills as fast as they were brought to him.

The steam drill had not been out long before John Henry thought he'd like to have a match with one.

So John Henry said to the captain:

"A man ain't nothing but a man,
But before I let that steam drill beat me down,
I'll die with my hammers in my hands, Lord, Lord,
Die with my hammers in my hands."

As his hammers flew back and forth ringing through the tunnel, John Henry's body glistened with sweat and shone as though it had been polished. The clang of his hammers was a high, steady chorus even above the sound of the steam drill as this giant of a man pitted himself against the machine. His boss and fellow workers stood watching. There had been some joking with John Henry before the match, but now everyone was silent.

For the first ten minutes the man and the steam drill seemed to be going at about the same pace. Then, little by little, John Henry began to pull ahead. There was one thing in his favor. Every so often the Burleigh drill would clog up on rock dust or hang up in a crack, and while the steam driller was taking care of this, John Henry went right on slinging those hammers—clang, clang, clang.

It was thirty-five minutes before the match was over and by that time John Henry had driven fourteen feet while the steam drill had driven only nine. John Henry turned to the steam driller and said, "Your hole's done choke and your drill done broke." The match was over and John Henry had won. But the big, proud, black man had trouble walking.

"I feel a roarin' and a rollin' in my head," he told Banks Terry, and he staggered home, laid down his hammers, and went to bed. The next morning he was dead. The feelings he had described are the classic symptoms of a stroke and few people nowadays, since the coming of power tools, can imagine such a brutal, man-killing contest.

Later, in 1876 a major rock fall killed a whole train crew, and a brick mason named Alfred Owens was one of those hired by the railroad to work in the tunnel and face it with brick. Owens had lived in the area all his life and been in the tunnel many a time as a boy. It was cold and damp inside it that November afternoon as he hurried to fit the last bricks into an arch and finish before he left. Only a half-dozen bricks remained when he heard a sound in the tunnel. A stray dog, a rat, or, worse, a rock fall, for in the great dark voids above the brick arching, blocks of rock shifted and fell with frightening frequency.

He hurried to put the remaining bricks in place, but as he did so, another sound rang out—a clang, clang, clang, clang nearby—and as he looked down the tunnel he saw a shadowy figure in the orange light of his lamp. It was the outline of a huge, strapping man silhouetted near the tunnel opening. In each hand was a hammer and the immense arms swung with smooth rapidity, never faltering, never losing their rhythm.

Owens was stunned. It was the entrance through which he had planned to leave. He edged toward it, pressing his back close against the tunnel wall while the loud clanging of the hammers striking steel went on and on. The air in the tunnel was cold, but Owens could feel perspiration running down his face. The palms of his hands were damp with fear. He became too frightened to move. A rock dislodged itself near his head and struck his shoulder, but even this did not frighten him nearly as much as the awesome figure swinging the hammers completely unmindful of him.

Then his foot slipped on the wet rock of the tunnel floor and he pitched forward almost at the very feet of—of what? An apparition? It could only be the specter of John Henry—once a living man with so much heart and so

Does the ghost of John Henry still haunt the tunnels of Appalachia?

much brawn he had dared to take on a machine and con-
quer it. Now, he had returned to the scene of his triumph.

Owens shook with fear, but when he managed to look
up, the figure was gone and the tunnel quiet. He was certain he had seen the ghost of John Henry. That night he
sought out the old man Banks Terry. He described what
had happened and Terry only nodded. Even now, some
say that the ghost of John Henry still returns to haunt the
Big Bend Tunnel. They say they have heard the sound of
his hammers and that his shadowy form stalks along
through the darkness, unmindful of the water that slowly
drips from overhead to form long and eerie stalactites.

A Visitor from the Dead

JESSIE JACKSON was a pretty blond girl whose husband was a miner. But John never seemed satisfied to stay at one mine for long. It always looked to him like the grass was greener elsewhere, and that is what sealed his doom.

When John and Jessie came to Grant Town, West Virginia, they moved into one of the mine company houses. It was a monstrous, creaky old place that the company hadn't been able to get anyone else to live in. The last miner who had occupied it years ago died in an accident in the mines and there was talk that the house was haunted. John just laughed at that. He told Jessie they needed all that space for the family they were going to have and he would fix the roof, the sagging front porch, and the rotten floor boards, and the house would be good as new. But Jessie, try as she would, never could seem to make the house look cheerful.

One winter morning Jackson took the lunch his wife had fixed for him and set off for work as usual. It was so cold he could see his breath curl in the air like tobacco smoke. Under his feet the ground was crisp and his boots slid now and then on puddles turned to dirty glass. He had some odd feelings on his way to the mine that morning and he mentioned them to his buddy, Tony Dominec. Although he had just left Jessie, it was like he missed her already. He couldn't understand why he felt so sad.

"You'd think you two was courtin'," joked Tony but he couldn't get a smile out of Jackson, who just shook his head and didn't say a word. They rode the buggy (a small locomotive used to haul coal cars), and when Dominec got off at his level he said, "Meetcha after work." Jackson, who was working one level down, nodded.

It was early afternoon when Dominec heard a terrible explosion in the depths of the mine. It seemed to come from beneath his feet and the men near him began running. He ran with them as fast as he could through the tunnel toward the main line. There he saw other miners racing through the main tunnel. Had a fire started on the level below? Would it spread? Would the main tunnel soon be filled with smoke?

Just ahead of him he saw men jumping into the buggy. His chest hurt, his legs felt as if they would give way under him, but he kept running and he managed to get into one of the last cars. When he reached the surface, he began looking for Jackson but he was nowhere to be found. By now wisps of smoke were coming out of the mouth of the mine.

The next morning there were knots of people standing around the entrance to the tunnel—the families of miners who had not come out on the buggy and several of the top men in the coal company. Jessie Jackson was there with her two little boys, waiting to hear whether the rescue crew that had gone into the mine would find any of the missing men still alive. Finally, they came out of the mine. They had found the place where the explosion had occurred, but the men near it had all been burned to death and John Jackson was one of them.

Times were hard and Jessie had only a little money to support herself and the two children. The spring after John's death she married Bill James, who had been one of her husband's close friends. Jessie would get up early, pack Bill's lunch, and off he would go to work at the mines. Then she would go back to bed for a while. About six months after her remarriage, Jessie began to see the ghost of her first husband. Each morning after she went back to bed the ghost would appear in a rocking chair near her. He would sit there staring for a while and then disappear. Jessie was so frightened she couldn't move. This went on for over a month, until she became more and more upset and had to be treated by the mining company doctor.

The doctor thought a change might be good for her and advised her to leave Grant Town for a few weeks and go home to visit her parents. When she returned, she and her husband moved into a new house about half a mile from her old home. Several weeks went by and much to her relief the ghost did not appear. But one morning she had just gone back to bed when she happened to look over at the rocker and there sat the apparition of her dead husband. She screamed and the specter disappeared, but the very next morning it was there again.

"What do you want? Tell me!" the terrified Mrs. James cried out.

The ghost motioned with his hand for her to come with

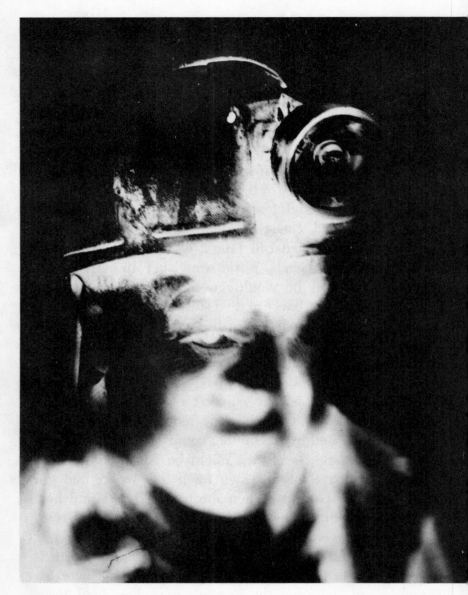

The ghost of John Jackson.

him. Upset as she was, she put on her coat quickly and began to follow the shadowy figure down the road. The ghost kept ten or fifteen feet ahead of her, drifting noiselessly but purposefully along, and there was no mistaking the fact that the spirit of her first husband seemed to know where it was going. Despite her fear she went on, and when the ghost turned off on the road that led to the mine, she turned, too.

As she arrived, she was just in time to see her second husband standing with a group of other miners waiting to get into the buggy that would take them into the mine. She called him over to her and explained how she had been led here by the ghost. Her husband became angry, for by now he thought all of this was some sort of foolishness. But Jessie began to tremble so, that he decided to take her to the doctor himself.

About lunchtime, when Bill and Jessie returned to the mine, they saw a crowd gathered around the entrance. Some of the women were crying as they held babies in their arms while others had children clinging to their skirts. Right after they had left, ten men had been buried in slate that had fallen from the roof of one of the tunnels, the very tunnel Bill James would have been working in that day. Jessie fell into her husband's arms and began to sob with relief.

If it had not been for the ghost of her first husband, her second would have died along with the other miners. They were both convinced that his ghost had returned from the dead to save Bill James's life, and from then on they placed flowers on his grave regularly.

The Ghosts of Shut-In Creek

THERE is a place near Hot Springs in Madison County, North Carolina, that's haunted, been haunted since I was a boy," said the white-haired old man.

"It may have started right after what happened to my uncle. He worked in a manganese mine up beyond Hot Springs at what they called Dry Branch. One mornin' they let my uncle down in the mine with the wooden box. He'd go down to the bottom, dig out manganese, and load it in the box until it was full and then they'd windlass the box back up.

"When a man would fill the box full, he'd shake the rope, and they kept waitin' and waitin' for my uncle to shake that rope but he never did. They began to holler down into the shaft and it was like a voice would holler

The cabin at Shut-In Creek.

up, but it was just their own calls comin' back at them. My uncle never did answer.

"Finally, they put hooks on ropes and let themselves down, and after awhile they managed to bring him up. But he was dead. Nobody knew for sure, but some said gas must have formed down there the night before and that's what killed him.

"They brought him up to the little old log house on the side of the mountain where he lived and they laid him out, a corpse. There was a real crowd there that night. Some sat inside with the body. Others just stood around outside the house. I took a turn sittin' inside. Always heard you ought to do that to keep the cats off the corpse, but the lamp in that room kept goin' out even after my aunt brought in a fresh cleaned one. That light goin' out began to work on me some, so I asked her to get someone else to take my chair and set a spell and I went on outdoors.

"We were all standin' around talkin' when someone called out, 'Looky there, comin' right down the mountain!' I looked and saw this big light. Then it started to roll over and over and it was big as a barrel. It was just a-rollin' comin' down toward us. It rolled over and over and over and everybody began to holler. But not my uncle's brother, Ben, and it was comin' at him p'int-blank.

"I don't know whether he'd been drinkin' or what, but he begun to curse that light with it rollin' off the hill toward him. And when he did, well, it hit him, knocked him down, and just kept on rollin' right down the side of the mountain and across the road. Some of them boys standin' nearby lit out runnin' and those of us that stayed 'cause we were too scared to move, we picked Ben up and took him inside. But he never did recover and he died later that night.

"He begun to curse that light with it rollin' off the hill toward him."

"The home place is still there near Shut-In Creek, and it's been haunted ever since. Comin' along that road through there at night certain times of the year, certain nights, you could hear people talkin'. I was comin' through there one night—my, it was dark—and I heard some people talkin' and it sounded like there was a passel of them. It was right near my uncle's house. I kept walkin' expectin' to meet somebody, but I never did meet anybody. I told

Shut-In Creek.

some folks about that later and a lot of people said, 'Why, I've heard that talkin' many a time.'

"You go about four miles beyond Hot Springs and then you turn to the left. That's Shut-In Creek and the haunted place is down aways about five miles. I wouldn't walk through there again at night, no matter what you gave me. They say the talkin' still goes on near that farm. You hear voices that seem like they move along the road right near you, but you never see a livin' soul."

Highway 19,
Where Apparitions Still Ride

THE driver of the truck tried his CB radio again.
"Breaker 19, Breaker 19, for north-bounder on Highway 19." Another West Virginia trucker's voice crackled
back over the CB radio. "You got a south-bounder. This is
the Big Driver." "How's it lookin' over your shoulder, good
buddy?" asked Craig Tolliver. "It's clean and green back
to Roanoke" came the reply. This was trucker's CB lingo
for the fact that there were no patrol cars, accidents, or
hazards over the stretch of road Tolliver would soon be
traveling.

He had heard some weird stories about this area. His
truck tended to hug the inside curve of the mountain road
for he knew that a steep drop lay to the left of his cab. A
few miles ahead was the hill that had brought death to

more than one driver—two of them truckers like himself. It was not the road itself that presented the hazard. It was something far more mystifying.

His big trailer truck began the slow climb up the hill. Why should he be so apprehensive? He had driven this road near Flatwoods, West Virginia, many a time and the trip had always been uneventful. Surely it was only chance that there had been more than one accident along here. The truck went more slowly than usual tonight. Did it too feel reluctant to reach the stretch of highway ahead? What foolishness, he thought. He was overtired, for there was always tension in driving a truck this heavily loaded, and the steel girders he was carrying weighed over twenty-two tons. No wonder the truck was slow to respond on the up grade and tended to hurtle forward as he went down the hills.

Tolliver strained to see ahead. Now he was approaching the crest of the hill. As he reached it, he saw a sight so amazing he could hardly believe his eyes. Halfway down the incline, in his lane, was a wagon pulled by four horses. On the seat was a man and beside him a woman with long hair wearing a white dress. He realized with horror that there was not a way in the world he could avoid hitting that wagon.

He was in low gear, and although he knew it was futile, he pressed the brake as hard as he could. As he went down the grade coming closer and closer to the wagon, his brakes began to burn. Why didn't the wagon turn into the other lane? It continued its slow and measured pace. He thought of trying to go around it but he knew the weight of the steel girders would send him hurtling over the embankment. He would never be able to pull back in his own lane ahead of it.

He knew in another half minute the couple and their

horses would all be one indistinguishable, bloody mass beneath the huge wheels of his truck. Tolliver felt a sudden wave of nausea and as if he were about to black out. In another second he would feel the impact. There was no way to avoid the collision.

Then, much to his astonishment, horses, wagon, and the couple all disappeared at the very moment he was braced for the impact! The moon came out and the road was illuminated behind him. As he looked in his mirror he could see that there was nothing there. What had happened? Where had the wagon and the couple gone? He knew that he had seen them as clearly as he had ever seen anything in his entire life.

It was only a short distance down the road to the truck stop where he had sometimes paused to refuel or for a cup of hot coffee. He needed that coffee tonight as he had never needed it before. When he lifted it steaming hot to his lips, his hands shook so that they spilled the coffee on the counter.

"You seem pretty shaken up, fellow, what's the trouble?" said a voice next to him. He turned to look at the man who had spoken.

"You a trucker?" he asked him. The man said, "No, I'm from over at Flatwoods, a few miles from here. Just thought I'd stop in and grab a sandwich."

Tolliver shook his head as if he would clear his mind.

"You know, if I didn't have good sense, I'd say I been seeing things and ought to be put away."

"What do you mean?"

Had it been another trucker he would have been too embarrassed to talk about it, but what difference did this old man make? He'd go back to the boondocks of Flatwoods, West Virginia, and nobody in his company would ever be any the wiser.

Truck drivers never know when the phantom will be around the next curve on Highway 19.

"You won't believe this, but comin' down that road a few miles back I was dead sure I was goin' to run right over the top of a wagon pulled by four horses." The man didn't look surprised.

"Was there a couple on the seat and the girl wearing a white dress?"

"There sure was," said the surprised Tolliver. "How'd you know that?"

"I've heard that story ever since I was a child. I was on that road one night when I was a young man on my way home from calling on my girl. It was bright moonlight and up ahead of me I saw an old wagon moving slowly up the hill. There was a man and a girl in a white dress with long yellow hair hanging to her waist. Their wagon was pulled by four white horses and it was loaded down with heaps of things like pioneers would carry. Those horses were milk white and when they came closer I could see they wore black harnesses with shiny brass studs. It was the strangest sight I ever saw. Just about the time I was close enough to hail them, that wagon disappeared and there was nothing on the road at all. It was a sight I'll never forget if I live to be a hundred. Every now and then somebody sees it. My grandfather told me when that road was no more than a trail, a young couple decided to settle up in here and they were on their way to camp for the night near Hacker's Creek when a band of Indians attacked and killed them, leaving their bodies beside the road.

"Every so often, when the moon is bright on certain nights, I've heard tell of that wagon being seen on top of the hill and it has caused some bad accidents there. Sometimes, I wonder about that couple, who they were and why they keep coming back."

The old man shook his head, drained the last drop from his coffee mug, and left.

The Mysterious Face on the Wall

NICK YELCHICK would have laughed if you had told him he would ever see a ghost. He was a big, strapping fellow who liked to brag a lot, and if he had too much to drink, it was better to stay away from him. After five years of working for the railroad, in March of 1927 he lost his job and began to find that the bottle helped him forget it. He would stop at a bootleggers in the late afternoon, have a few drinks, and then head home with his own jug.

Whenever he was drunk he would get angry over trifles, beat his wife, and tear up the house. This went on for several months. In the daytime he went out looking for work and finally was able to get one of the West Virginia mines to take him on.

The first week everything seemed to go well. The hours

were long and the work took plenty of physical strength, but that didn't bother him. He had always made friends quickly, and although the other men would wink at each other, when Nick started bragging, most of them liked him. And, at home things were better because he wasn't drinking.

But on Friday at lunch he asked one of his buddies to punch his timecard for him after work that afternoon for he wanted to get to his liquor supplier. His friend promised to do so.

Nick sat down to eat his lunch, and as he was eating one of the sandwiches Anna had packed for him, he began to think of some of the other tunnels where the men had been working that might be easier to mine.

He went down to the level below his own tunnel and inspected the walls as he walked. Other tunnels led off the main one and he turned down one of these, then down another and another before he realized he had lost his way. Aware he was lost, he began to panic and try desperately to get back to the main line. He had walked for several hours when the thought struck him that nobody would be looking for him because he had asked his buddy, John Avangio, to punch his timecard for him. No one would know he was still down in the mine.

After he had walked until what must have been late that night, his light burned out. Now he was in total darkness and he lost his self-control, shouting and shouting until his voice became a whisper. He knew he should wait until morning but he couldn't stop. Finally, he was so exhausted he was too tired to walk any further. He slumped down against the wall of the tunnel and fell fast asleep.

He was awakened by a strange dream. He had dreamed that he saw his wife's face before him and as he stared into the blackness he saw a luminous spot gradually take

*Nick Yelchick left the safety of the main tunnel and went
down below, inspecting the walls as he walked.*

shape on the wall of the tunnel and his wife's face stared
back at him. He put his arms across his face, convinced
that he must still be dreaming, and then he heard her voice
and she was saying, "Follow me." Her face began to move
along the wall of the tunnel and, frightened though he
was, he managed to get up and walk toward it. The eyes
shone out at him and the lips seemed to move again form-
ing the words, "Follow me, follow me."
Down one tunnel and then another he went, the face

staying just ahead of him. This went on for what must have been over an hour until, at last, he found himself on the main line once more. He looked for the face but it had disappeared. When he arrived at the surface of the mine the night watchman said, "What you been doin' down there, Nick? Your wife was here lookin' for you yesterday, but I seen your card was punched and I told her you had left."

When Nick got home, the first thing he saw was his wife lying across the bed. He went over to wake her, thinking she must have been up all night. When he shook her she didn't move, and then he realized she was dead. On the kitchen table he found a note that said, "Nick, I thought you would stop drinking when you got this job but now I know better."

Nick Yelchick collapsed in a chair, and with his arms on the table he began sobbing, for he knew now that it was his wife's ghost that had come to lead him out of the mine and save his life. From that day on he was a changed man, until he died in Grant Town over twenty years later.

The Specter's Vengeance

A few hours before John Lyons had loaded up the last of his ore at the Copperhill Mine at Ducktown, Tennessee. His blond hair fell over his eyes as he hunched forward, feeling the pull of his team of horses, for the load was a heavy one. He was a good-natured young man and the money he was making hauling ore would soon be enough for a small farm for himself and the girl in Kingsport whom he planned to marry. His mind dwelt happily upon these things.

But the ride to the river was not to be the quiet one he had expected and his musings were soon interrupted by apprehension.

Robbers had been waylaying wagons near here and driving the horses and wagons over the cliff after robbing

After robbing the bodies of the dead drivers, the robbers would drive horses and wagons over the cliff.

the bodies of the dead drivers. Lyons, like most of the teamsters in eastern Tennessee and North Carolina, was well paid for hauling ore from the mine to the river dock. He patted his money belt uneasily, and as darkness fell across mountains and valleys, every shadow seemed ready to leap out at him.

Thinking he heard sounds other than the creaking of his wagon wheels, he looked around expecting to see robbers at any moment. It was not his imagination, for another wagon was following his. Acting on impulse he decided to pull over into the woods and let it pass. As he waited, he saw it come into view in the moonlight. It was loaded high with copper ore and on the seat sat the figure of a huge man. The fellow wore a dust-covered jacket, secured by one button, and a broad-brimmed, black felt hat.

Lyons stared curiously at the face, and at first glance was appalled by its pallor and staring eyes. But as he watched, the features seemed to spring to life. The mouth broke into a smile and the hollow eyes lit up. The features were strangely familiar. The man obviously meant him no harm and it was good to have company on this road, he thought gratefully.

But not far away from the landing on the river, where the boats were loaded to carry ore to the smelter in Chattanooga, the band of outlaws was already lying in wait. They stood well back in the brush along the banks of the creek where the road from the mine crossed it. Whispering and grumbling they waited.

"I told you John Lyons would be the last teamster away from Ducktown tonight. Poor fellow, hauling that last lonesome load of copper to the landing," their leader smirked. But his words froze on his lips as he watched the wagon cross the ford. Neither the horse's hoofs nor the wagon wheels splashed the placid surface, but, instead, the wagon appeared to glide over the water.

"Must be turrible low water over that rock," one of the men said. Another spoke up. "Look at that driver, boys. Recognize him, Lem?"

"I think so, but I can't say for sure. He looks strung out, don't he?"

While they watched, a second wagon appeared and took the ford almost in one leap without a call to the horses or a splash. Just as the leader of the robber band raised his pistol, a third wagon appeared. The robbers by now were

He concealed himself in the woods and watched the wagon pass.

thoroughly bewildered, for they had expected only John Lyons. Almost as much in fear as to signal the attack, the leader pulled the trigger.

His men swept down, encircling the doomed wagons. In the manner Indians attack, they galloped in a circle around them. Almost in slow motion the three teamsters reached into their wagons and pulled out their rifles, each aiming in a different direction. Before they could fire, the encircling band of outlaws cut loose with their six-shooter revolvers.

The report of gunfire echoed off the mountainside and three of the robbers lay dead from their own bullets. A moment later the wagons vanished as if they had never been there and the night was quiet. The silence was suddenly broken by the sound of a teamster whip and yet another wagon rolled along, heading for the ford. The driver drove it with a certain bold abandon and a broad smile upon his face as he headed straight for the landing.

The remaining two outlaws were stunned. Surely, this must be Lyons' wagon and now things would go their way. They began emptying their revolvers at the driver who cracked his whip repeatedly in some sort of wild exultation.

He smiled gleefully as bullets whizzed toward him and his crackling whip gave off tiny sparks in the moonlight. "Keep on firing, boys!" he shouted. His whip touched the tree branches and sent them shivering and rustling. As John Lyons watched from a safe distance back beside the road, he thought he saw the tip of the whip stroke each branch and the leaves sparkle like Fourth of July fireworks. Red and gold bursts of flame, followed by tiny sparks, floated down, struck the rocks in the stream, and faded into extinction. Then all was quiet, for the last of the robbers had fled.

The ride to the river was to be more terrifying than John Lyons could ever have known.

John Lyons was filled with awe. He had recognized some of the drivers of the wagons that passed him, but the reason for his astonishment was that they were all dead! They were the drivers who had been murdered here during the past two years. If it had not been for them, by now he too would probably have been murdered. His life had been saved by a phantom wagon train.

The Angel of Death

P ATTY MCCOY was chilled to the bone, but it was not the September night as much as the words she had just heard: "Beware of the cemetery gates, for they will bring death!" She was terrified, for the gates of the cemetery were opposite the McCoy house. The only light in the room came from the kerosene lamp. The witchwoman's skin was seamed and leathery. One eye stared fiercely straight ahead and the other veered off into space with a fiercely malevolent look.

"I see you as a child full of joy," said the woman. "Then as a young girl, when you first met your husband. You wore a blue crocheted shawl the night he asked you to marry him. Isn't that so?" Patty nodded. "He's still a likely-favored man. Is he not?" Patty's eyes filled with tears at the thought of him sitting at sundown on the porch, his banjo in his lap, playing the tunes he loved. He had been ill for almost a year and that was the reason she had come here for advice. Today Bradley was to go to the hospital.

"There is one thing you must never let happen," warned the old woman in her rasping voice, head thrust forward. "I know your homeplace well and the gates of that cemetery are right across the road from it. When they take him

Strange plants grew around the witchwoman's home.

to the hospital, don't you let them open that gate. If you do, he's going to die. For what's inside those gates will never rest until it gets him."

Patty put her hand over her mouth to keep from screaming. People had always said, "That Patty. She ain't afeard of nothin'." But now she was afraid. She put a fifty-cent piece in the woman's hand and left.

All she could think about was whether they had come yet to get Bradley. She had been gone for almost two hours. The witchwoman had prepared bits of bone, feathers, roots before she would tell her what to do about Bradley. Patty had no sooner reached the edge of the woods and the open field across which she could see the house when she gave a shriek. For out in front of the porch was a small, dusty ambulance to take him to Louisville. She began to run. Her breath came fast and her heart pounded. She was halfway up the road to the house when the front door opened and two men bearing a stretcher with Bradley carried it down the front steps and placed it in the back of the ambulance.

She screamed out at them, "Wait! Don't take my Bradley 'til I tell ye about the gate." The men looked at her strangely but waited. Now she stood beside them and for a moment was too breathless to warn them about what the witchwoman had told her. She looked at Bradley lying so still on the stretcher, his face the color of putty.

"Kin ye holp him?" asked Patty. The ambulance driver, a tall, red-haired man with watery blue eyes, looked down at her expressionlessly and nodded.

"Well, there ain't no turn-around up here," said Patty. "And when ye git that ambulance down to the road, whatever ye do, don't open the gate of the cemetery to back in. Do ye hear me?"

The driver and his helper got in the ambulance and

"The thing inside those gates will never rest until it gets him."

Patty watched as they backed it down the narrow mountain trail. When they reached the road they must have tried three or four times to back and cut sharp so the ambulance could head out. One of the men finally stood by the side of the road hollering at the other, "If'n you'll just open that gate, we won't have no trouble." But Patty had taken down the shotgun from over the fireplace just as a precaution, run down the road after them, and now stood squarely in front of the gate.

The driver of the ambulance looked at her and at the

shotgun, cut the wheels of the ambulance hard, and this time he made it. Patty stood with her back against the cemetery gate and watched the ambulance until it was out of sight. Then she turned and gazed down the road and up the hill toward the cemetery. It was dusk, and as she looked up toward the markers on the crest, she shuddered. What could possibly be up there that could harm her Bradley? A wind sprang up rustling the tree leaves. It felt chilly for this time of year. Patty shivered and watched the shadows from the cypress trees begin to merge into the coming darkness. Then she turned and walked up the road toward home.

A week later she went to town with Joe Hartley and they brought Bradley back from the hospital in his old pick-up truck. Bradley looked lots better and talked like he felt pretty good, but by the time he was jounced all the way home in the truck, Patty saw he was tired. He wouldn't lie down none though. Said he had to get out and hoe their fall garden. She saw he just needed to do something, so she let him be.

Bradley acted like he was tired a lot of the time and he was a little "tetchy" which wasn't like him. Before he always let her know he was sorry if he saw something he'd said discomfited her, but he didn't talk much now and seldom said anything about the future, like how he was going to buy the land next to theirs and clear it or build another room on to the small cabin nor did he ever hug her about the waist as he used to do and tell her she was still the "likeliest favored gal" he ever saw.

Less than two months later he was down in the bed again, so tired that the littlest thing seemed to make him too weak to lift his head. The doctor wanted him to go to the hospital and Patty wanted to try to get him on the mend at home, but finally she agreed that he should go.

She waited with Bradley, holding his hand until the ambulance could get there. It was a large, new ambulance this time, but the tall, white-faced, red-haired man got out with a little, short, chesty fellow who looked well able to handle a stretcher even with a big man on it. Patty pushed back a strand of hair that lay across her husband's forehead and then with a jerky, self-conscious motion bent down and kissed his cheek. The men put the stretcher in the back of the ambulance. Patty felt like she was going to cry, and, turning, she went into the house. She heard the slam of the two doors as the men got in the front and the quiet purr of the motor as the ambulance started backing down the road.

Then, she flung herself across the patchwork quilt on the old walnut bed, but she couldn't cry. Her chest hurt and began to heave. She lay there holding her arms tightly around her and shook, but no tears came.

Suddenly, she recalled the gate and what the witch-woman had told her. She was out the door in an instant and running down the rutted trail that led from the house to the road, when she saw the short, heavy set man jump out of the ambulance and start for the gate. She screamed with all her might, but the wind only blew the words back at her. The gate swung open, the ambulance backed in, and was out and gone. The autumn sunlight struck its massive chrome front and nearly blinded her.

She ran toward the gate, pulled it closed, and then leaned on it, looking toward the hill where the bodies of relatives, friends, and parents were buried. She had not been able to keep the gate closed even after what the witchwoman had told her. Patty leaned against it, feeling as if she was going to faint.

Now the wind sprang up with a vengeance. The leaves that had been green and tender two months before when

The wind sprang up with a vengeance and the last of the leaves rustled like sandpaper on the day death claimed Bradley McCoy.

she had stood at this gate made the harsh, rustling sounds of sandpaper rubbing together, like the eerie rasp of the witchwoman's voice saying over and over, "Don't let them open the cemetery gate! Don't let them open the cemetery gate! Don't let them open it!" The voice within her grew more and more shrill until she felt that she was floating on a sea of madness. Bradley, Bradley . . . she knew she had failed him.

On top of the hill stood a small knot of people huddled together to escape the biting wind of the winter day. It was the graveyard prayer for Bradley McCoy who had died in the ambulance on the way to the hospital. Patty stood near the grave, head bowed.

She was convinced that something had come out of this cemetery three days before. Some dark, stalking thing that refused to be thwarted and it had claimed Bradley McCoy.

NANCY ROBERTS is best known for her books on Carolina ghosts, but has also done a half-dozen other books including WHERE TIME STOOD STILL: A PORTRAIT OF APPALA-CHIA, which was selected as one of the outstanding books for young people in 1970 by both the *School and Library Journal* and the New York *Times*.

Her other books include THE GOODLIEST LAND: NORTH CAROLINA and SENSE OF DISCOVERY: THE MOUNTAIN, as well as GHOSTS AND SPECTERS, AMERICA'S MOST HAUNTED PLACES, and GHOSTS OF THE WILD WEST, written for young readers.

BRUCE ROBERTS' photographs have appeared in many national publications. He has twice been named Southern Photographer of the Year. Among his previous books are THE FACE OF NORTH CAROLINA and THE CAROLINA GOLD RUSH, AMERICA'S FIRST. In addition to ghosts, he photographs people.